Natkha the naughty Monkey

Retold By:
Namrata Gupta

Illustrated By:
Ajay Kumar

PANDA
An imprint of Unicorn Books

Natkhat — the Barber

*Natkhat —The naughty Monkey

ISBN 978-81-7806-101-5

© Publishers

UNICORN BOOKS Pvt Ltd.

J-3/16, Darya Ganj, New Delhi-110002
Phones: 23276539,23272783/84, Fax: 23257790,
E mail: unicornbooks@vsnl.com
Website: www.unicornbooks.in • www.kidscorner.com

2

Natkhat* found a box
containing barber's kit.

3

He decided to open a
barber's shop in the jungle
and earn some money.

Natkhat
Barber Shop

4

Kaloo, the Bear, had a problem.
He had too much hair,
he had hair in his nose,
he had hair growing out of his ears,
his hair fell over his eyes.
All he could see was hair.

When he talked, he got a mouthful
of hair in his mouth.
When he walked, he tripped over his
hair.

Kaloo went to Natkhat, the new barber, for a haircut.

"Sit down," said Natkhat. He was happy to have a customer.

"Don't worry, Mr Kaloo," said Natkhat. "I'll cut your hair just right. You'll know what you're eating, you'll see where you're going."

He took out his biggest pair of scissors and a large comb. He climbed on Kaloo's shoulders and began to cut his hair.

8

Suddenly, a bird flew out of Kaloo's hair. Natkhat almost fell off Bhaloo's shoulders.

Then he saw a nest in Kaloo's hair. The nest had many little birds in it. Natkhat took the nest out. Then, he started cutting Kaloo's hair again.

11

Suddenly, a squirrel ran out, and then two butterflies, three rats and a pair of frogs with big blue eyes.
Kaloo was a walking zoo!

Kaloo was sleepy. He
closed his eyes and started
snoring. The job was taking too
long. Natkhat began to get sleepy too.
Natkhat's eyes began to close as he kept on
cut-cut-cutting Kaloo's hair.
Now up, now down, now left.........

13

Suddenly, Natkhat woke up. Kaloo looked strange. He didn't have a single hair left!

14

What would Kaloo
do when he woke up
and saw himself?

In fear, Natkhat
climbed up a tree.

He climbed right to the top of
the tree.

Kaloo, the Bear woke up and saw a
funny-looking pig in the mirror and
started laughing too. Then he realised
he was laughing at himself!

Seeing Kaloo laughing, Natkhat also
began to laugh.

Kaloo burst into tears. "Look at my bald head. Everyone will call me 'Baldy'.

" Natkhat jumped down and said, "Don't cry. I will give you a beautiful turban."

18

He tied a beautiful red turban on Kaloo's head.

"No one will see your bald head now," said Natkhat.

Kaloo, the Bear, was
happy. He could see
and hear and
he could walk and talk.

Kaloo, felt like a **King!!**

Natkhat — the artist

Natkhat, wanted to be an artist.
He dreamed of a day when he would
be a famous artist, the greatest in
the world.

Natkhat started working hard so that his dream might come true. He practised and painted from morning to evening. He painted sunrises and sunsets. He painted flowers and trees. He even painted his own face. At times, he even forgot to eat his meals.

23

He used all the colours he could find. He made paintings of all shapes and sizes. He made big paintings and small paintings, round paintings and square paintings. He did this because he knew people had different tastes.

Natkhat displayed all his paintings on the pavement. He hoped people would rush to buy them. But no one bothered. Everyone just hurried past him.

"Silly people, they don't know a great artist when they see one," Natkhat thought.

Natkhat wanted to prove himself. He wanted to be famous. He went from door to door to see if anyone wanted his or her house painted.

Natkhat found a box
of paint and brush in
a house.

"This is my chance. People can't
miss this big house with my
paintings on it. I'll be famous,"
Natkhat thought.

Natkhat started painting. He painted a sunrise and a sunset. He painted a rainbow on the roof and his own face on the front door.

He said, "My! That's beautiful!"

When he had finished, he called the lady of the house to come and look at all the paintings.

She was not at all pleased.

Instead of being happy, the lady grabbed a big paintbrush and hit Natkhat on the head with it.

Natkhat ran away as fast as he could.

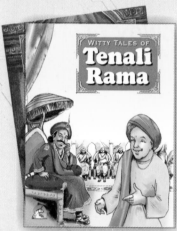

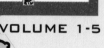

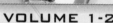